DIVE INTO READING!

The Protest

Henry   Lily   Mei   Pablo   Padma

by Samantha Thornhill

illustrated by Shirley Ng-Benitez

Lee & Low Books Inc.   New York

Dedicated to the dreamers —S.T.

To the Benitez family, and to friends everywhere
who peacefully assemble for the rights
of the greater good —S.N-B.

LEE & LOW BOOKS Inc., 95 Madison Avenue, New York, NY 10016, leeandlow.com
Book design by Charice Silverman
Book production by The Kids at Our House
The illustrations are rendered in watercolor and altered digitally
Manufactured in China by Imago
Printed on paper from responsible sources
(hc) 10 9 8 7 6 5 4 3 2 1
(pb) 10 9 8 7 6 5 4 3 2 1
First Edition

Library of Congress Cataloging-in-Publication Data
Names: Thornhill, Samantha, author. | Ng-Benitez, Shirley, illustrator.
Title: The protest / by Samantha Thornhill; illustrated by Shirley Ng-Benitez.
Description: First edition. | New York: Lee & Low Books, [2021]
Series: Dive into reading! | Audience: Ages 4-7. | Audience: Grades K-1.
Summary: "Lily and her friends organize a protest in order to save their
neighborhood public garden from being demolished" —Provided by publisher.
Identifiers: LCCN 2020021772 | ISBN 9781643792088 (hardcover)
ISBN 9781643792095 (paperback) | ISBN 9781643794730 (ebook)
Subjects: CYAC: Protest movements—Fiction. | Community gardens—Fiction.
Classification: LCC PZ7.T3934 Pr 2020 | DDC [E]—dc23
LC record available at https://lccn.loc.gov/2020021772

Contents

Bad News

Lily and her mom walked
to the public garden to see
their neighbor Mr. Sam.

Mr. Sam was not watering
the plants as usual.

"Are you okay, Mr. Sam?"
asked Lily.
"No," said Mr. Sam.

"We have to close our garden.
Some builders want to make our
public garden into a parking lot."

"The city is changing fast
with new people and buildings,"
said Mr. Sam.
Lily frowned and looked around.

It wasn't fair to close
the public garden.
"Can we save the garden?"
asked Lily.
"We can try," said Mr. Sam.

Lily shared the news with her friends Padma, Pablo, Mei, and Henry. "What will we do after school without the garden?" asked Mei.

"Where will our school get vegetables for lunch?" asked Padma. "Where will I get strawberries for breakfast?" asked Pablo.

"We need to protest the closing of the garden," said Lily.
"But we're just kids!" said Henry.

"Hey, we *kids* grew enough
vegetables to feed our school
at lunch," said Padma.
"Kids can do a lot!" said Lily.

Bright Ideas

Lily thought about how to protest. People could call their neighbors. People could make posters.

People could invite reporters.
Lily decided to plan a rally
to save the garden.

Lily shared her plan for a rally
with her friends and parents.
"Good idea, Lily!" they said.
They planned to hold the rally
in one week.

Lily and her friends told
their neighbors about the rally.
Together they would protest
the closing of the garden.

Then the friends met at Lily's home
to make posters for the protest.
Henry brought poster boards.
Pablo brought rulers.

Mei brought markers and glitter glues.
Padma and Lily thought about
what to write on the posters.

After they finished the posters,
they needed a chant.
"What should we say?" asked Mei.
"No cars, no! Let our garden
grow!" said Lily.

No cars, no!
Let our
garden grow!

"Great chant, Lily!" said Henry.
Now they were ready for the rally.
Lily hoped others would join them.

Rally Day

On the morning of the rally, Lily, her friends, and their parents waited outside their building.

It looked as if no one else
was coming to protest.

But then neighbors, kids from school, and their parents came to protest.

Lily and her friends were happy.

Everyone started walking
to the garden together.
Everyone held their posters high.
"No cars, no! Let our garden
grow!" everyone chanted.

More neighbors joined the protest.
The crowd grew larger.
The chant grew louder.

Finally everyone arrived
at the garden.
A reporter came to the rally.
The reporter asked Lily
about the protest.

Then Mr. Sam got a phone call.
The crowd became quiet
and listened.

Mr. Sam said the builders would
wait until next year to build
the parking lot.
The people had saved the garden!